Sharing

By Gloria J. Rayborn

Illustrated by Aleshia Strong

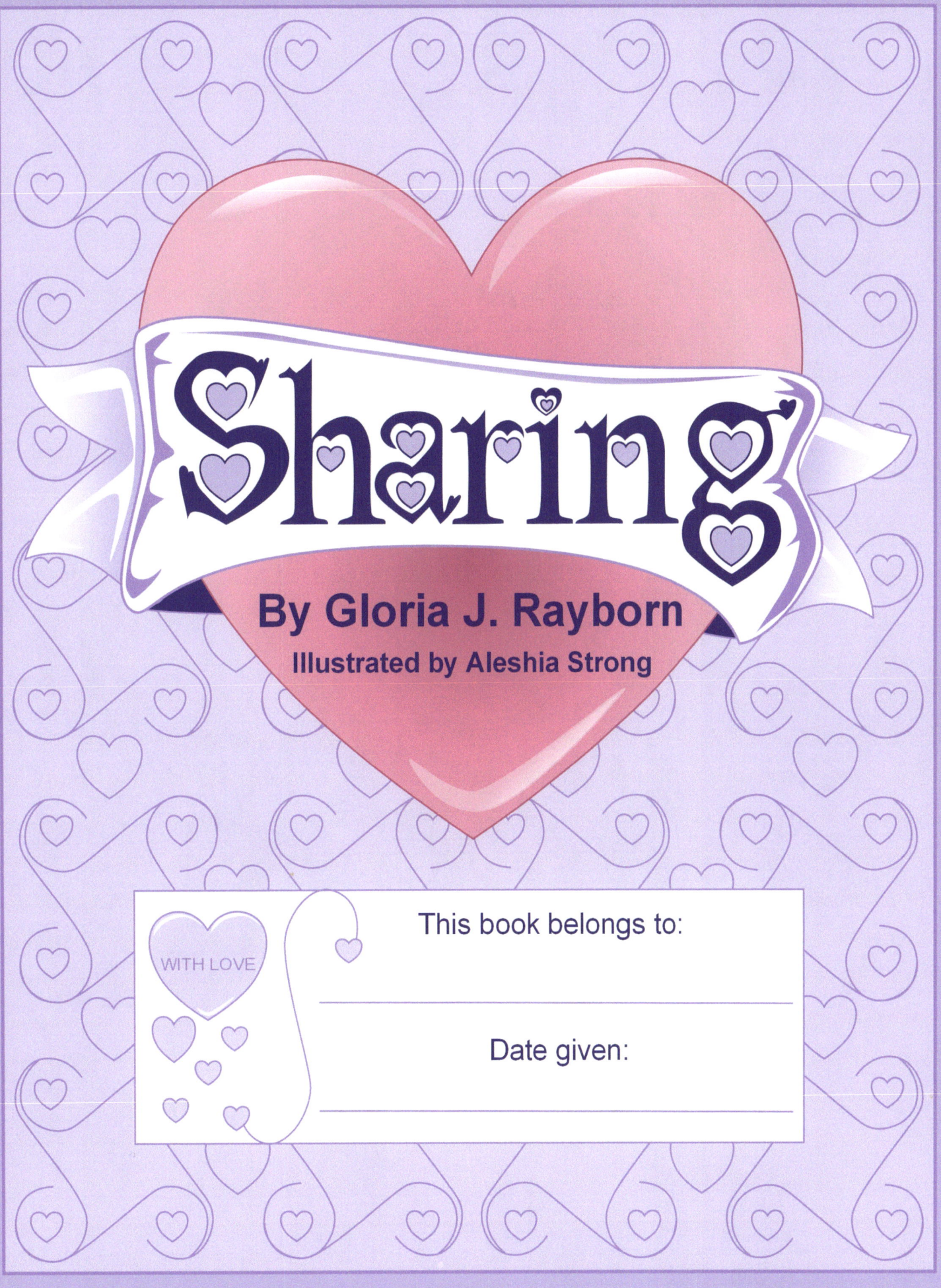

Sharing

By Gloria J. Rayborn

Illustrated by Aleshia Strong

WITH LOVE

This book belongs to:

_____

Date given:

_____

Victoria and her friend Mya

like to do things together.

They run, they jump, they dance, they sing. They jump, they play, they do all sorts of things.

Sing

Dance

They see each other whenever they can, because they are the best of friends.

Sometimes they even dress alike. They do everything with all their might.

One thing they don't do very well is share their toys.

In this sense they are like lots of girls and boys.

When they play they each have their own: Two dolls, two brushes, two sets of clothes,

Two combs, two sets of crayons at each of their homes.

One day Victoria and Mya went to play with Reese and Aly

And there was only one tricycle
for them to ride.

Reese and Aly wanted to ride and ride and ride.

Victoria and Mya wanted a turn but couldn't,

and so they cried and cried and cried.

 Reese's and Aly's Moms asked the girls what was wrong.

They said Reese and Aly wouldn't share and that made them sad.

Reese said it was her tricycle and had been bought by her Dad.

Reese's Mom said that each girl should take a turn.

Riding the tricycle was a lesson they could each learn on how to share when there was only one toy,

And how sharing would bring them each lots of joy.

So Victoria and Mya
learned a lesson that day
That sharing is what they
should do when they play.

Taking turns and sharing
is a good thing
It makes friends happy
and let's their hearts sing.

I share, you share, we share!
Sharing is fun because we love
each other and because
we care.

© Gloria Rayborn 2017

Books by Gloria J. Rayborn :

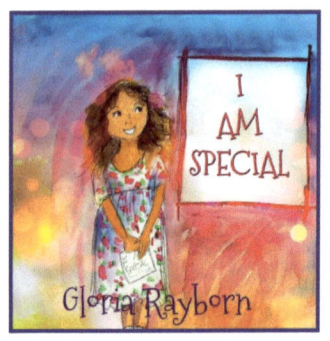

"I AM SPECIAL"

"Let's Go On A Treasure Hunt - Searching For Hidden Treasure"

"HANDING DOWN A LEGACY OF BLESSINGS: THINGS I WANT YOU TO *KNOW* WHAT I HOPE YOU WILL *BE* & THINGS I HOPE YOU WILL *DO*"

"Sharing: Learning to Share"